A Tropical Bear Learns To Surf

Text and art by Lloyd Berardy

Gopher Press

Honolulu Hawaii

www.TropicalBearHawaii.com

There's a place in the ocean all sandy and green
A tropical place, if you know what I mean.

It's a land that is filled with warm summer things, Like hiking and swimming
and hammocks that swing. And people all over come visit this place,
To sight-see and suntan and enjoy the slow pace.

Look under that tree, there's a
polar bear there.
A large happy fellow with
fluffy white fur.

This bear came here and decided to stay
To enjoy the sunshine
and the ocean's salt spray.

He wasn't raised here in the
tropics and sun,for the place he
came from was a place that had none.

Pip is his name, he's a bear with white fur. His size is so big that he causes a stir.

"The sun and the ocean's the reason I'm here. A sky that's so blue and the water so clear.
My home has blue sky's with water and such,
But the wind often blows and the sun don't shine much."

"I've tried many things since I came to this land
Like swimming with fishes and laying in sand."

"I've learned many new things from daybreak to sunset,
I've learned how to sun bathe,
I've learned how to sweat."

"I've learned about shopping as all tourists do,
I've been about shopping till my feet are blue."

"I've learned to dance hula, with leis and grass skirts,
I've swung my big hips till my big old back hurts."

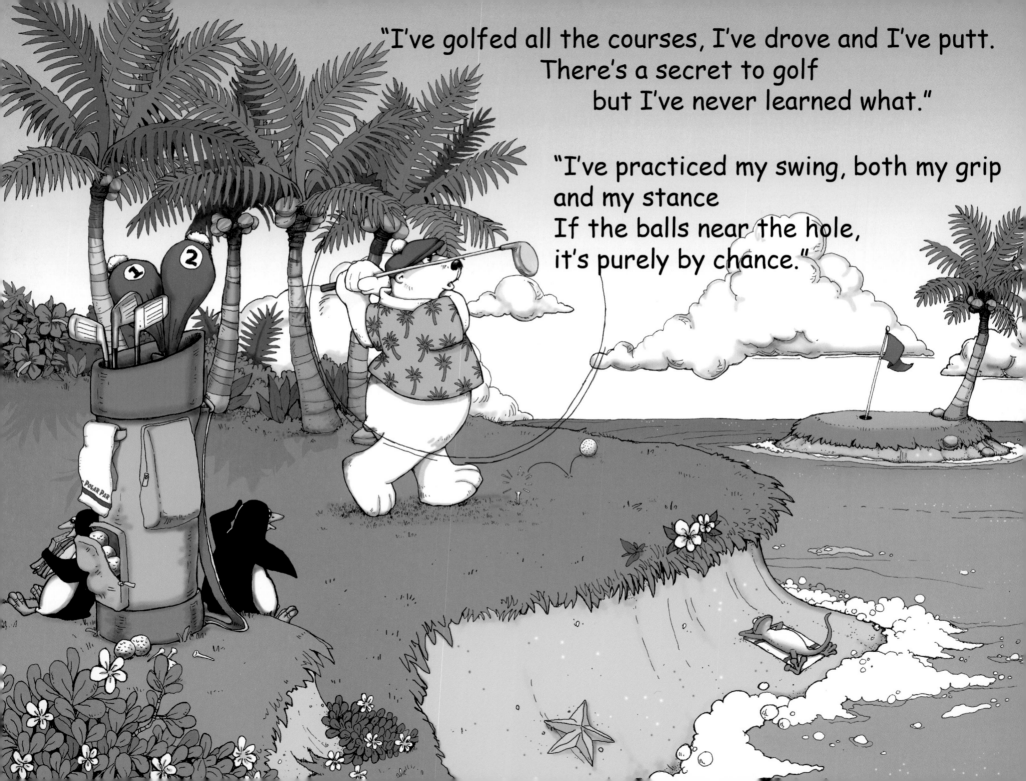

"Today is a new day, I'll try some new thing
Like fishing or sailing or maybe surfing."

"I should ask my friends to help me to learn
Their guidance is good and won't be too stern."

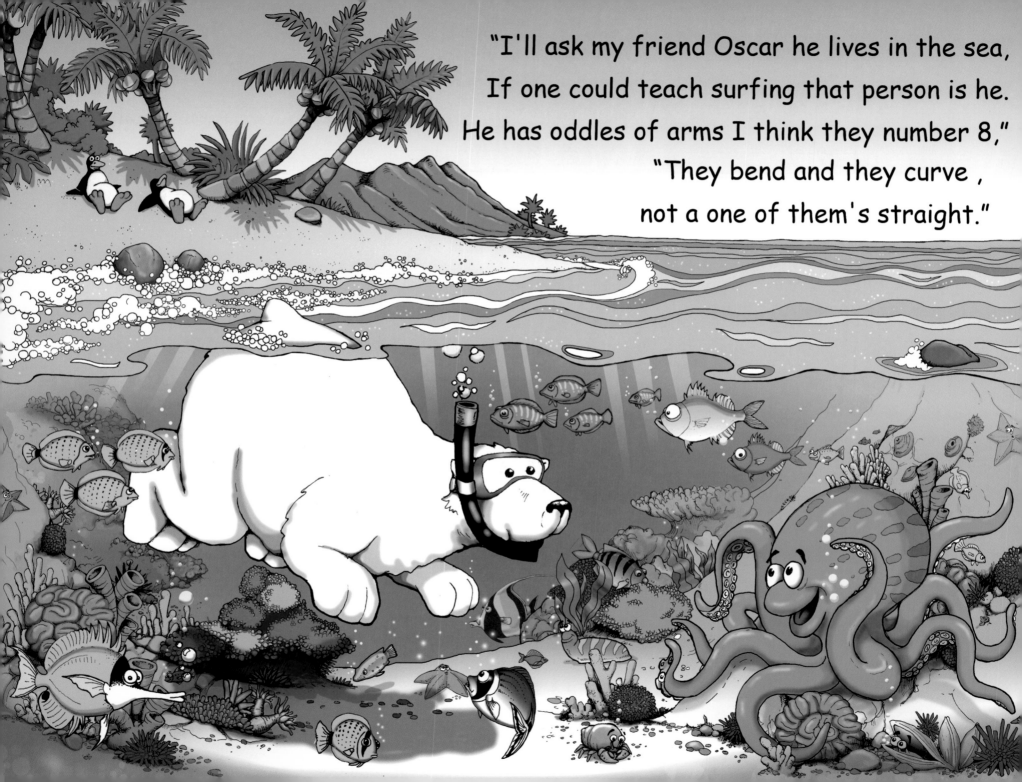

"I'll ask my friend Oscar he lives in the sea,
If one could teach surfing that person is he.
He has oddles of arms I think they number 8,"
"They bend and they curve ,
not a one of them's straight."

"Of course, we will teach you, we surf all the time. We slide on the wave tops, we turn on a dime.

"Come with us Pip friend and we'll start your first lesson.
It'll be fun to see a big bear in a turtle surf session."

"Now the first thing to do is take off your hard shell

then jump up on top and let out a big yell."

Pip stood there and watched
as his heart fell and fell
For he looked back and saw
he was missing a shell.

"Well, this just won't do,
their style just won't fit."
For I don't have a shell
on the place where I sit."

"Well thank you dear friends
for this kind demonstration,
to show me your skills
while I'm on my vacation."

"I think I see now
how to move on the wave,
How not to be frightened,
how one should be brave."

Then Pip went in search of another surf teacher,
for someone to teach him no matter the creature.
And then he remembered a bird tall and all white,
a kind, but odd fowl he saw practicing flight.

"Why just yesterday I met a
                    strange chap,
His feet were all blue and his
                    long wings did flap.
He said he was aquatic since
                    he was a chick,
That he could teach surfing,
                    I'd pick it up quick."

"Well coming to me Pip was definitely smart,
I'll teach you in no time...let's see...where should we start?"

"Place your left leg like this...
tuck the other one here,

stretch out your wings on both side,
now stick out your big rear."

Pip tucked and he stretched and he stuck out his big rear,
Then he fell with a splash.

thank goodness the ocean was near.

"Well thanks for your time, Bob,
but I can't get it right,

it may be my big feet
or my cumbersome height."

So Pip took his board and
went back to his shack

"It's balance and grace
and good timing I lack.

"A bear just like me finds it hard to do things,
Without 6 more arms, a hard shell or long wings."

"Hey there Pip, you seem to be down in the mouth, We'll teach you to surf, we're the best in the south."

"Where we come from there are none to compare,

we'll teach turtles or birds or even white bears."

"First pick out a board that is right for your size,
Make it big, make it strong,
one that floats would be wise."

"Try these shorts on dear friend,
we don't mean to be rude,
But surfing bare here
is considered quite crude."

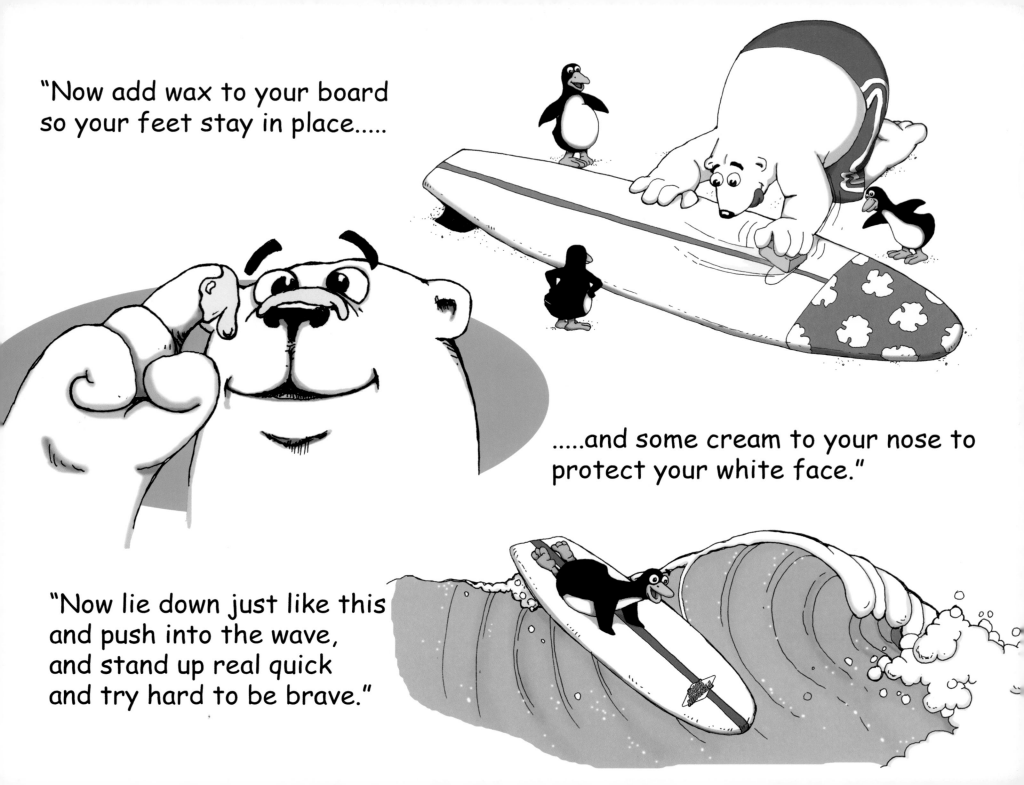

"Now add wax to your board so your feet stay in place.....

.....and some cream to your nose to protect your white face."

"Now lie down just like this and push into the wave, and stand up real quick and try hard to be brave."

So Pip took a big breath and soon followed their lead,
He pushed into the wave and took off with great speed.

He jumped to his feet and he bent at the knee
As his good friend Oscar
had said was the key.

Then he stuck out his rear as Bob said to do,
And found that his balance had greatly improved.

And he let out a yell
as the turtles had done
And found out that surfing
was really quite fun.

He zipped and he zoomed
he had fun without doubt
He was wet, he was happy,
he tuckered right out.

Having used all the pointers his good friends
could teach. He paddled his surfboard
right back to the beach.
"The things that they taught me
helped me to succeed,
Each style so different
but useful to me."

For Oscar's strange style worked just right for him,
Whether surfing a wave or taking a swim.
And Bob and the turtles had tricks all their own
That helped them to surf well,
not sink like a stone.

Then tired and happy his day was at end
Pip learned a new lesson , to value his friends.
And as the sun set and they sat down to eat
He thanked them for friendship, a friendship so sweet.

A Tropical Bear In Hawaii Series:

A Tropical Bear In Hawaii

A Tropical Bear Learns To Surf

A Tropical Bear Underwater

To order these titles for friends and family
please go online at www.TropicalBearHawaii.com

Also see our line of Tropical Bear gift items

To contact the author please email lloyd@tropicalbearhawaii.com